A Daughter is for Life

Jenny Telfer Chaplin

Jenny Telfer Chaplin

Published by Kinnon Enterprises Ottawa

© Jenny Telfer Chaplin 2012

ISBN 978-0-9698825-3-4

ONE

When young Kay Caxton opened her eyes that early morning in the Spring of 1968 it was to the realization that this was the day to which she had long been looking forward. As she stretched luxuriously back in the comfort of her cosy bed she thought: *It's here, I'm sixteen today and life's looking good.*

Suddenly her nose twitched as catching the unmistakable and life-enriching aroma of fried bacon, she smiled, eased herself back into a sitting position and thought: *Any minute now good old Dad is going to appear with a mug of tea for me in one hand and a ketchup-lathered bacon-butty in the other. Yes, life's looking better all the time.*

As her beloved, home-on-leave from the high seas, Dad handed in the cordon-bleu breakfast he grinned and said: "Get that down you, Kay, Then come and see your birthday fan mail."

The bacon-butty, tasting every bit as delicious as it had promised, was hardly eaten before she clambered out of bed. Pausing only long enough for a fleeting glance in the dressing-table mirror at her post-breakfast image she then headed at high speed to the lounge. With a barely audible, good morning, flung at her mother, Kay grabbed up the waiting pile of mail.

As she did so her mother's return greeting was by way of the inevitable reprimand.

"Kay, for goodness sake have you seen the sight of you? Could you not wipe that disgusting smear of sauce off your chin? Anyone would think we're living in a slum. And at least draw a comb through your hair? It is your birthday after all and as I pointed out when I woke you earlier at the first time of calling, here you are now poised on the threshold of adulthood."

Kay pressed her lips tightly together then opening them barely wide enough she muttered: "Yes, Mum, I know it's my birthday. Why else do you think I've got all this fan mail?"

Her Dad looked from one to the other of the two women in his life, then in a joking tone of voice, said: "Right girls, enough of this gitterin-on. While it's true that you do in fact look rather like the popular image of the Bride of Dracula on a bad hair day, one thing we're all agreed on, it is your birthday. So how about your cards?"

Obviously glad that yet another family slanging match had thus been so skilfully averted, her Mum, trying hard to match the mood of carefree jollity and good camaraderie, gave a tinkling laugh together with the words: "So far as I am aware the Queen does not send birthday greetings to sixteen-year-olds. But having said that there is one rather official looking envelope in that bundle."

No sooner were the words spoken then Kay jerked her head round. "Oh, that's charming I must say. You must have been raking and nosey-parkering your way through my private correspondence."

Her Dad shot her a look and in a mock-warning voice said: "Any more of that snash my girl and you'll be lucky to make it through long enough to reach your seventeenth birthday."

As the shared, tension-relieving laughter died away and feeling the eyes of her parents already boring into her, Kay got to work in ripping open all the envelopes. That done she gave a cursory glance at each flower-bedecked birthday card, made a mental note as to which of her many friends and relatives had sent the sugar-sweet greetings, then without further ado she tossed the cards away, aiming somewhat nonchalantly in the general direction of the long low G-plan coffee-table.

On the point of opening the last envelope she turned to face her Mum when the latter said: "Kay for goodness sake, girl, I don't think that is very nice. To toss aside those cards to hang up on the floor. After all, people, including your grandparents, spent good hard-earned money on buying such lovely expensive cards. And what about the cost of postage and so on?"

Kay bridled and determined to give as good as she got, snapped: "Look Mum it is my birthday. My cards. And for your information I'll do what I damned well like with them."

A Daughter is for Life

A sudden intake of breath from her Mum indicated to Kay that her barb had shot home. Then ignoring all warning signs and at the same time pressing home her supposed advantage, Kay said: "Anyway you can keep your school ma'am voice and admonitions for the Lower Fourth, at least there the School Governors pay you for your efforts."

Another intake of breath, then as her Mum opened her mouth to reply Kay's Dad was first to enter the fray. "Now then, Kay, you know that is no way to speak to your Mum especially after all the trouble she has taken, in fact trouble we've both taken to mark this special birthday."

Kay pulled back in surprise at thus being reprimanded by her beloved Dad then said: "Um er, look, I'm sorry, Dad, but the thing is you still don't know just how very special today can be. If you could both just give me a minute's peace to open this last envelope. But the way the pair of you are going on at me you're in danger of spoiling my day and also my big surprise."

Her Mum's face flared an angry red. She got to her feet.

"It's more than your day that's being ruined. And irate school-ma'am or not I personally have had all the surprises I want for one day, thank you all the same."

As her Mum headed towards the door she was stopped in her tracks when Captain Jim, apparently immune to the finer nuances of the ongoing domestic drama being played out around him, asked in all seeming innocence: "What's for lunch?"

That comment was enough to light the fuse wire of Janet's housewifely frustration.

"If it's lunch you're after, why not forage for it yourself? Nobody cut off your legs. You can find the kitchen as easily as I can. What's for lunch indeed."

As Mrs Caxton departed in a flurry of self-righteous fury, the crashing of the door behind her said it all.

In the silence which ensued in the wake of her dramatic exit, Kay and her Dad raised their eyes to heaven. Then, as their eyes locked in a meaningful glance, with the hint of barely suppressed laughter in his voice, the gallant ship's Captain said: "Well, no surprise there, Kay. So I think we can take it, that beyond the shadow of a doubt, that's our lunch now well and truly out of the window."

Having delivered himself of this conclusion, Kay's Dad stretched out his slippered feet on the nearest pouffe, settled back more comfortably in his armchair, grinned like a naughty schoolboy and said: "Right then, daughter of mine ... are you opening that envelope or not? And perhaps even more to the point how's about throwing all caution to the winds and opening your birthday box of chocolates?"

At these words, Kay already inwardly regretting the unwarranted verbal attack on her Mum, chewed at her lower lip. "Yes, but what about Mum? Don't we have to wait till she comes back?"

His eyes already feasting on the beribboned box of chocolates, the sweet-toothed ship's master shook his head.

"Uch, Kay, we both know what she's like. Just leave her be for the time being. Anyway, since you ask, I'd like an orange cream. On second thoughts be a love and just pass me the box."

As her Dad intently studied the chocolate box menu, Kay took the opportunity of a moment's respite finally to tear open the rather official-looking envelope, already knowing full well that the letter would contain no surprises for her. Even so in seeing with her own eyes the official confirmation of the momentous event in type below the important letter-heading ... suddenly it brought her dreams into the here and now and so into the realms of life-changing reality. Then without further ado, and interrupting the luxury of his private chocolate heaven, Kay rushed over to her Dad and tried to thrust the official letter into his chocolate-bearing hands and said: "Dad, Dad read this."

He smiled. "As you can see, I've got my hands full at the moment, so why don't you read the letter to me? Anyway, my fingers will be all chocolatey, so go on pet, you read it."

Kay needed no second bidding and with the captive audience of her beloved Dad gazing up at her, she cleared her throat. Then in a voice which could barely conceal her excitement she began: "Dear Miss Caxton, Following your recent successful interview for the post of Junior Medical Secretary to Professor Brian Sutherland within the University's Faculty of Medicine, we are pleased to offer you the situation. Full details with regard to terms of employment etc will be forwarded to you on your formal acceptance of this offer. Yours sincerely, etc."

TWO

Having cashed her first-ever salary cheque and having borne home in triumph the visible fruits of her labour, Kay smiled with pleasure as her mother complimented her.

"Oh well done, dear, well done. You know, I may not always put it into words but the fact remains I am really very proud of you. Just wait till your Dad gets home on his next leave and hears what a success you're making of your first job. He'll be proud as a peacock."

Kay blushed in the glory of such rare praise. With not a harsh word having been spoken between them now for days on end, in that moment of parental praise and approval she felt inspired to say: "Mum, with my first pay now a reality, please tell me how much I should be contributing to the household purse. And how much would you suggest for my pocket money? If by some miracle, there's then anything left over, what I'd really like to do is to buy a special memento, an ornament or some such for you and Dad."

No sooner had Kay finished speaking than glancing over she could see her Mum's eyes had filled with tears. This was confirmed when before replying Mrs Caxton had to swallow hard. Finally, in a voice quite unlike her usual school-ma'am authoritative tones she said: "Kay, you really are a very caring, good girl, aren't you?"

Kay uncertain as to how to reply to such fulsome praise being heaped on her, instead said nothing and waited for her Mum to continue speaking.

In a voice still choked with emotion her Mum said: "With regard to the divvying-up of your hard-earned money, for this first-ever momentous salary, here's what I'd suggest: why don't you head for the shops tomorrow, buy a small inexpensive trinket for us, then keep the rest of the cash for yourself?"

The Saturday morning shopping expedition duly over and her Mum declaring herself perfectly entranced with the Hong-Kong manufactured musical cigarette-box, Kay then said: "My friend Bettina has asked me to go with her to her college dance tonight. That all right with you Mum?"

Mrs Caxton pursed her lips. "What about Gary? Won't he be escorting you?"

Kay shook her head with such vigour that a lock of her long blonde hair fell like a silk curtain over her brow.

"Gary taking me out? Hmph. No, thing is, he's hardly speaking to me after that recent Wendy House fiasco. If you must know, seems it was all my fault, first of all for taking him along on a baby-sitting assignment and then secondly my dastardly plan to belittle him by letting two wee girls run wild to the extent of making him their prisoner."

Mrs Caxton shook with laughter. "So, one way and another, I suppose that poor old Gary is now what you might call past history?"

Kay nodded. "But to get back to tonight, Mum. Bettina's Dad has volunteered himself to drive us to the dance and then home again. But with your permission, of course, perhaps I could even stay overnight at Bettina's. Her mother says it would be all right with her."

Mrs Caxton clearly still in a good mood with her mental image of young Gary, the teenager's Mr Wonderful, as the tied and bound captive of a pair of ringletted five-year-old twins, smiled.

"Stay overnight at Bettina's, of course that will be perfectly all right with me. No better way to celebrate your first salary ... just one proviso, however ..."

Kay raised her eyes to heaven and gave a barely audible 'tut'. Although well-attuned to such peevish signs of discontent, for once Kay's Mum chose to ignore such blatant insubordination, as she also totally disregarded the muttered comment: "Knew it was too good to last. Here we go. Okay, let's have it."

A Daughter is for Life

In a flurry of excitement and girlish giggles Bettina and Kay made their perfumed way into the overheated dance hall with Kay clutching her new embroidered handbag. They settled at a table a fair distance from the band, but in full view of the group of available young men. The two girls chatted earnestly as though not the least bit interested in the feet-tapping, eyes-roving, smartly suited callow youths.

Determined to show off her new handbag, Kay made a great performance of opening it to retrieve her lace-edged handkerchief.

Seeing this Bettina chuckled. "Well, if your dear Mum told you to leave safely at home the rest of your money and your house keys, is that trendy new handbag, which I've just happened to notice ... is it just for swank? Apart from holding your toothbrush and a clean pair of knickers, of course for tomorrow."

Kay smoothed back her curtain of hair. "Listen, pal of mine, what my dear Mum tells me to do and what 1 choose to do are two entirely different things."

Bettina grinned. "Well, in that case, if you're the one in funds, no need to wait for some guy to treat us to an orange squash. Since you're paying, think I'll go mad and have an iced drink ... vanilla, if they have it."

Early next morning, with the Sunday streets as yet empty of churchgoers, and again back home, Kay pressed the doorbell of their family bungalow. As the sound reverberated through the hall beyond the door, Kay could then hear her Mum's footsteps hastening to admit her.

With the door wide open, her Mum at once greeted Kay with the conventional words of greeting: "Did you have a lovely time dear? Was the dance well attended? I hope you remembered to thank Mr and Mrs Spence for their kind hospitality."

When Kay uttered not a word in reply but gazed soundlessly at her Mum, this caused the latter's conversational flow to stop.

"What is it? What's the matter, are you ill? Kay, answer me, please do not tell me ... you did take strong drink and even after all I said."

Kay let out a pitiful wail. "Oh Mum, please, please don't be angry with me. It's nothing to do with drink, strong or otherwise, but the thing is ... what happened was ... it was my bag, my lovely new handbag. Somebody stole my bag."

Far from being annoyed at hearing this revelation, instead her Mum patted Kay's arm.

"There, there dear calm yourself. Of course I'm not angry, why on earth would I be? So some sneak thief stole your bag, hardly your fault and upsetting enough I know, but we can soon get you another one. After all, it isn't as if you had anything of any value in it, panties and a toothbrush are easily replaced."

When Kay made no response, her Mum sought further to reassure her. "As I say I'll be happy to treat you to a new bag, a leather shoulder one perhaps, a bit less flamboyant. It's just a good job you did as I suggested before you left and placed your money, diary and house keys safely in your vanity case in your bedroom."

Another long drawn-out wail escaped Kay's lips.

On hearing this there was a moment's stunned silence, then her Mum grabbed hold of both arms and pulled Kay towards her until when eyeball-to-eyeball, she finally said in a hoarse whisper: "I take it you did follow my advice?"

Another silence then like an angry fish-wife her Mum bawled: "Oh no. you stupid, stupid girl. And after all I said."

As a paroxysm of weeping shook Kay's body her Mum ranted on: "Wait a minute, please don't tell me – do not tell me you also had your diary with your name, address, phone number and your teddy bear key ring with ... God help us ... all the house keys?"

A wild look in Kay's tear-streaked eyes told its own story.

Then shaking her daughter like a floppy rag doll, Mrs Caxton screamed: "Even worse, you mean to say, all this fiasco happened last night. That meant alone in this unprotected house as I was, some maniacal cut-throat wandering the streets with my house keys could have let himself in and attacked, raped, even murdered me in my bed. Dear God in heaven, you left me alone, vulnerable and at the mercy of any axe-wielding murderer. Yet you didn't even think to phone and warn me of such possible, imminent danger?"

Struggling to free herself from her mother's vice-like grip, Kay screamed: "It wasn't like that. Mr Spence did phone. He phoned the police. They said, best not to alarm you unduly at that stage, especially that late on a Saturday night."

"Alarm me unduly? Love of God, somebody should have warned me to be on my guard."

Kay mopped at her still gushing tears. "But the police, very understanding, said time enough to give you the bad news when I'd got home today. After all, they reckoned it was highly unlikely the thief or thieves would strike immediately. Be more likely to case the joint first, phone up to find out if the house was empty or –"

Mrs Caxton stared wild-eyed. "Oh sweet Jesus. The phone did go very late on last night, I actually thought it might have been your Dad speaking from his latest port of call in America. But when I answered there was no-one on the line."

Just at that, a ringing at the doorbell caused them both to jump like terrified rabbits on the run. Mrs Caxton opened the door to admit two uniformed policemen. Later on, sitting in the lounge, these guardians of law and order explained in detail that just having come from the grounds of the college, they had found a variety of empty, abandoned handbags hanging from the trees and bushes, for all the world like a riot of colourful summer blossoms. They then went on to detail what the householder must now do with regard to the immediate changing of door locks. Helpful as ever, they gave details of a 24-hour emergency locksmith. They further explained that in the interim period while waiting also to change the telephone number, the house occupants should no longer, on any account, reply to any call by stating the designated house telephone number. Finally, as they rose to take their leave, the younger of the two policemen let it be known, as a sort of throwaway comment: " Sorry to add to your problems, Mrs Caxton, but we should also warn you that reliable and quick as he is, that all-hours emergency locksmith does not come cheap."

With her mother's meaningful look in her direction, Kay knew precisely who would be getting the bill for any such specialized service. She also had a gut feeling as to where her next month's salary, not to mention any baby-sitting pin money, would be going. As she sat enveloped in a dark cloud of misery, remorse and the blackest depression, her tearstained eyes alighted on the memento cigarette-box. She choked back a cry of despair.

"I'll remember all I ever need of this disaster without the sight of any cheap trinket to remind me. Talk about growing up? Life in the real world? Who needs it?"

THREE

Life as Junior Medical Secretary to Professor Sutherland was not without its highs and lows, and it had a carried-over-by-association sense of superiority in being the left-hand aide of such a noted academic. One of the privileges which went with the job was that of being entitled to use the full facilities of the staff leisure-centre with its splendid squash courts, restaurant and swimming pool. Fully appreciative of all this and especially in view of her current financial penury, Kay had taken to enjoying a complimentary Sunday morning swim, followed by a poolside mug of bargain-priced hot chocolate. This particular day as she sat at one of the tables luxuriating in the clammy warmth of the pool area, she mentally relived the entire bag-snatching nightmare. Suddenly, she became aware that a woman, having taken the chair opposite was now speaking to her.

With head cocked on one side, Kay said: "Sorry, did you say something. I was miles away."

The forty-something woman smiled. "You certainly were, in fact, almost on another planet by the look of you I'd say."

Kay grinned. "I sometimes think my Mum wishes I could be at such a distance from planet Earth, especially when my Dad's at sea and she's the only one in charge."

The attractive woman laughed. "Before you say another word, my dear, to incriminate yourself, I am at something of an advantage, you see I already know who you are. Please let me introduce myself, I'm Diana Sutherland. Your Prof's ever-loving."

A Daughter is for Life

Introductions over, the blonde-haired woman went on: "I must tell you, since Brian employed you there's never a day goes by but that he comes home bursting to tell me the latest amusing tale."

Kay could feel herself blush. "Oh, you mean those horrendous muddles I get into when having struggled with my certificate-winning shorthand I get about one word in twenty of the Prof's dictation and then present the poor man with a garbled version of what he'd really said?"

Diana Sutherland laughed. "Well, yes, there is that, of course. But then ... and this is classified information, I may say ... my husband actually loves your wonderful sense of humour and how you can take a joke against yourself."

Kay fiddled with her mug of chocolate. "Thank you for telling me that Mrs Sutherland. I can't honestly say I was aware of that."

Her table companion grinned. "Something to do with corporate staff discipline, I imagine. Anyway, apart from that, take for instance the time you were taking dictation in the ante-room of the operating theatre, The way my husband tells it, it seems you took one horrified look at his blood-encased boots, made a pithy comment about Sweeney Todd, the Demon Barber and his drumming-up business for the undertaker. Then like some jittery, wrapped-in-cotton-wool, over-corseted Victorian maiden you swooned gracefully, as to the manner born, into the waiting arms of the anaesthetist."

Kay gave a sheepish laugh. "Oh I'll never ever forget my introduction to operating days."

Diana grinned. "And neither will my husband. In fact, I must tell you, he dined out on that particular story for weeks on end."

Kay could f feel herself blush and to cover her discomfiture, she fiddled with the fringes of her bathing towel as she waited for Prof's wife to go on.

"And then there was his famous speech on Open Day, let us not forget that, the copy of which important speech you had typed up like some sort of anagram compilation and then handed to him just as he went into the lecture-room to give his annual address on medical matters to the great British public."

Kay chuckled "My Mum, she's a headmistress, you know, she was in the auditorium that day, said she could see the eminent Professor struggling to refrain from laughing each time he consulted his sheaf of lecture-notes. But when she found out that it was none other than her own darling daughter who had prepared the typewritten pages, she didn't find it all so amusing then. Far from it, in fact, all hell broke loose in our family home. She fully expected the Prof to sack me for that particular lash-up, as she would have done had it been any secretary of hers."

Diana threw back her head and laughed. "Sack you? Not a bit of it. Kay, I rather think my husband looks on you as a sort of substitute daughter. We lost a little girl to bone cancer, you know. Anyway, I think he sees you as a young girl, straight out of college and still struggling valiantly to distinguish between the spellings of such diverse medical terms as coronary botulism, osteoporosis, renal dysfunction and, of course, not forgetting that rather dreary chap of your own invention ... a certain Mister Arthur Itis."

They both laughed, then Mrs S. leant forward. "All that aside, Prof tells me that sometimes you and your boyfriend can be persuaded into a spot of baby sitting?

Kay nodded, hoping this might be a harbinger of good luck in the pin money stakes Then true to form and always ready for a giggle, even at her own expense, she rushed in to say: "I expect the Prof told you, when Gary and I babysat the other week for Doctor Young and his wife, their twin-girls ended up a night of riotous fun and games by locking Gary in their Wendy House."

Diana nodded. "I believe I did hear something of that particular exploit."

Kay grinned. "Just about everybody in the Faculty had a chuckle at that one. By now, it's probably gone into the annals of the entire University."

Diana rose to her feet, wrapping her rainbow-coloured bathing towel around her. Then leaning an elegant hand on the table she said: "Well, if you and your boyfriend are interested in babysitting for us, the good news is ... it's three boys we have and with not a Wendy House in sight. And even should they feel inclined to imprison Gary in their tree house, by now with Gary's track record, no doubt he'll be a master of escapology, don't you think?"

Kay too rose to her feet and said: "As to that, Mrs S I've no idea as to Dave's skills as a gaol-breaker, he's my new boyfriend, but I'm sure he'd be happy to join me in a spot of baby sitting."

"That's settled then, I'll be in touch well before the Faculty anniversary dinner. And please do keep up the good work in the office and in the ante-room of the operating theatre. You're a real breath of fresh air, the Medical Faculty has never known anyone quite like you. Now, I must dash, 'Bye for now."

FOUR

The short winter day was already fading and whereas other people were switching on table lamps, turning up the heating and generally snuggling down for an evening of home-comfort, by contrast in the Caxton's house, the atmosphere was one of icy coldness as Kay and her mother yet again were locked in a fierce family row.

"Kay, I cannot believe how utterly stupid you have been to walk out of the prestigious Faculty of Medicine with imminent promotion on the horizon. A job where, despite spells of the utmost incompetence, you are obviously regarded as a valuable member of staff, indeed from what you tell me, almost as a substitute daughter to your boss and his wife. Not to mention, a very suitable situation where day and daily you are meeting and actually socializing with eligible young doctors, up and coming professors and brilliant academics, all very suitable prospective husband material. To leave all that; leave it all on a whim, it really does beggar belief."

Kay laid down her coffee cup with great deliberation. "Listen, Mum, if you must know, truth of the matter is, I actually handed in my official notice a month ago."

"You did what?"

"So as of now, as of today. I am a free agent and whether you like the idea or not, I am perfectly at liberty to apply for any job I wish. And it just so happens, that I've set my sights on becoming an air-hostess."

Mrs Caxton's eyes widened in astonishment

"First I've heard of any such ambition. Now you tell me you've handed in your notice to a prestigious job; handed it in a month ago without so much as single word to me or even a letter to your father and ..."

Kay broke in, "For goodness sake, Mother, even you can see, surely, since I got the job by own efforts in the first place, why shouldn't I do the same, act independently, when I wish to leave it?"

Her mother glared at her. "All very well in theory I suppose, but not to say a word, not a single hint as to what you're doing or planning. Doesn't courtesy come into it at any point? Of course, had your beloved Dad been home on leave, that would have been entirely different."

Kay gave a mocking tilt of her head. "As a matter of fact, I did write an airmail to Dad, but I don't know if it will have caught up with him yet or not."

Although her mother opened her mouth to speak, it was several minutes before she was calm enough to do so.

"Listen my girl, first thing Monday morning, I shall phone from my office and try to contact Professor Sutherland and try to get you reinstated and then ..."

As her mother's words trailed off, Kay got to her feet. "You'd be wasting your time, Mother, it would be utterly pointless. They've already given me a farewell tea-party and wished me luck in my new career. The general opinion seemed to be that I have the figure and the legs for the snazzy uniform."

Her mother gave an annoyed tutting sound. "The uniform? I should think you're still a very long way from that, my girl. You cannot just march into a job like that, there are such things as interview panels, training and the like. I don't suppose any of that actually occurred to you, now did it?"

Kay gave a self-satisfied smirk. "The good news is I've already got an interview lined up for such a post. I'm to go to their offices in London next week, so now you know."

Mrs Caxton drew a trembling hand over her brow. "You call that good news? Dear God, this gets worse by the minute. You mean to say, all that expensive education, the exclusive secretarial school, with costly equipment, designer uniform ... that is to count for nothing and all for you now to be dead-set on becoming a sort of airborne, glorified cafe waitress. Dealing with difficult, drunken passengers and handing out sick-bags. Not quite as romantic as you seem to visualise it all, is it?"

Kay flushed an angry red. "If you must know mother, quite apart from the people at my farewell tea-party, all of my friends and I do mean all of them, they say I'm smart enough and glamorous enough to wear the snazzy uniform. Even my ex-boyfriend when I bumped into him in town the other day, even he was generous enough to say that I've definitely got the legs for it."

Her mother got up from her chair. "Not quite the way I'd have put it as the essential qualification for the job of becoming a trolley-dolly, unless, of course, he meant the miles of walking up and down the aisles of a plane dispensing booze to already sozzled folk."

A silence fell between them until her mother said: "Anyway, leaving your long legs out of it, I'd be rather more inclined to say that you've taken leave of your senses. I just cannot imagine what has possessed you or where you are coming from on this hare-brained notion. From what I could see you were making a real success of your life here. A great job at the University, an excellent social life, a comfortable home. Oh, I know you and I have many a row, often over nothing at all, but I guess that's all down to hormones, yours as a teenager and me with the mood swings of the Change. Kay, don't go to that interview in London. At least if you must get another different type of job, why not try for ..."

"Oh, Mum, please, can't we leave it?"

"Leave it you say? If only we could stop there. You know, I just do not get a good feeling about this. It's given me pause for concern. So far as I know, there's no insanity in our family, but perhaps it has to start somewhere, so why not with you."

Kay recoiled in horror. "Mother, that's a terrible thing to say to me. Another thing that may not have occurred to you ... perhaps my wanderlust, mibbe that's inherited from my Dad ... after all, as you say, things have to start somewhere and Dad once told me that there had never been any other seafarer in his family, so why not think along those lines instead of giving me a whole lot of grief and utterly useless negative thought?"

When Kay arrived back from her interview, she told her mother: "Yes, the travel firm have given me a job, but not as an air hostess my eyesight let me down on that. But they've offered me a post at one of their hotels in Majorca, as a children's holiday rep, I'll be organising leisure activities for them, doing baby-sitting, all that sort of thing. I'm really looking forward to flying out to the sun."

Her mother pressed her lips tight together. "A job in the sun, well, dear, I suppose we'd better get into town and get you some new summer clothing; tweed coats and winter boot not much good in Majorca, you agree?"

For the next couple of months, Janet was able to tell her friend Elsie: "Yes, thank goodness, she does seem to be making a go of it out there, so I hold my hands up and say that I may well have overreacted when the idea was first sprung on me.. But then, you can't help but worry about your children, now can you? I know you're exactly the same with your family, and it's all boys you have, I'm sure that must be easier."

Elsie gave a hearty laugh. "Easier, not my word for the world of teenage angst over every spot, girlfriend trouble, exam results ... need I go on?"

The two friends laughed. "Mm, I see that, just a different set of problems. And let's not forget that old saying, something about .... let's see now ..."

Together to the amazement of the passing waitress in the Kardomah coffee-house, the two middle-aged women started reciting: "A son's a son till he gets a wife, but a daughter's a daughter all her life."

Elsie smiled. "I think we both deserve a fresh coffee and perhaps one of their delicious little cakes after that feat of memory, don't you?"

As the two women later parted, agreeing to meet up the following Saturday morning, Janet said: "I'll give you a phone before then and let you know the latest thrilling instalment from Majorca ... she's learning to speak Spanish, you know, all very commendable, but from what she tells me she's made some really embarrassing mistakes in trying out her 'prentice hand at fluent Spanish."

Elsie patted her arm. "No shame to that, do you remember when we were trying out the Dutch language, on that exchange visit, 'Milk of Magnesia was what we wanted from the pharmacist for the children and what did we end up with? – moisturising milk among other things. Only one way to learn another language is speak it, wade in, warts and all and learn as you go along. See you next Saturday."

FIVE

The dreary days of November were dragging slowly to month's end and already people were beginning to make plans for the coming festive season. As Kay was being helped down the aircraft steps and into the terminal, she was surprised to see her mother at the front of a press of people all waiting to meet friends and relatives.

"Mum, what a lovely surprise. But how on earth did you know I'd be arriving back from Majorca today?"

Her mother gave a puzzled frown and Kay caught the look she exchanged with Aunt Elsie, her mother's best friend from their college days.

But it was Elsie who said: "As far as I know, it was the senior holiday rep who phoned your mother, gave her some sketchy details of your accident and so on, told us your flight number, so here we are to welcome you back. Anyway, all that matters is you're here now. Your Mum and I have been standing about here all morning, what with your plane being delayed. I don't know about your Mum, but I for one am simply dying for a warm cup of tea. So what say we make a move and quick about it?"

As the trio left the terminal building, for the next stage of the journey home, Kay turned her head in surprise as first of all her mother took hold of one arm, then Aunt Elsie grabbed hold of the other. As the two friends thus escorted her like some decrepit octogenarian, Kay meanwhile puzzled as to what on earth was going on.

"Good heavens, what a fuss about nothing. I shudder to think what that damned holiday rep told you, Mum. It was a fall, nothing more. I'm not injured in any way. All right, so my head got a helluva wallop, but that doesn't make me a cripple, now does it? One minute I'm the star of the show; the best children's rep they've ever had, they told me, and the children loved me. We all had great fun, enjoying beach games, treasure hunts, disco dancing and all in the lovely Spanish sunshine. A wonderful lifestyle. And next thing, here I am back in freezing cold miserable old UK being treated like a pensioner, as if I'm incapable of walking on my own."

Almost as if her Mum had read her thoughts and now aware of the violent shivering of Kay's body, she said: "Kay dear, wrap my cardigan round you, I brought this extra cosy one along. No wonder you're shivering, in those lightweight summer clothes."

If the month of November had been bad, it was as nothing compared to the disaster that was the so-called festive season. With it being one of the coldest winters on record, Kay was less than inclined to venture out away from the centrally heated comfort of the family bungalow. To make matters worse, not only had Captain Jim after a brief few day's leave, sailed from Liverpool on Christmas Eve, among the family's Christmas mail, was a letter from the company to say that Kay's services as a junior children's holiday rep were no longer required. The letter went on to point out that her contract with them had been on a strictly trial basis and the trial period had now expired. However, she should feel free to re-apply at a later date, and meanwhile, they wished her the Season's Greetings.

The cold unforgiving days of January were well established and any day now her Mum was due to get started to the new school term.

One morning Kay had been especially reluctant to leave the comforting warmth, safety and security of her bed and bedroom. All for what? To face the misery and trauma of yet another day still dreaming of the wonderful lifestyle she'd had in the sun-kissed holiday island?

Her mother eventually announced: "More than high time you were up, my girl, this ridiculous carry-on just is not good enough, it isn't helping either one of us."

A Daughter is for Life

Kay peered up from the sanctuary of the mound of blankets and eiderdown. "Why should I get up? Nothing to get up for, no job, no friends, no sunshine; Dad somewhere on the high seas, just the misery of a damp, bone-crippling British winter."

Her mother, hands on hips, stood at the side of Kay's bed.

"Not a very uplifting list, I do agree and most of which I personally can do nothing about. There is one thing however which I can change, so out of bed with you, smart like, and for heaven's sake draw a comb through your hair, it looks as if it hasn't seen a brush in days. Get dressed, quick as you can and come into the lounge, you and I, my lady are going to have a talk."

Kay groaned and made to turn her body round in bed to face the wall. This at once prompted her mother to lunge forward, grab her daughter's shoulders and say in a voice that brooked no argument, "Ten minutes, my girl, not a second longer, or so help me, I'll drag you out of bed even if I have to call in the police, the army, or the fire brigade to help me."

As the time limit expired and ignoring all orders about hair-combing or even getting dressed, Kay slopped her slipper-footed way into the room where her entrance was greeted by a despairing look from her mother and the cry: "One thing doesn't change; you always look like you've been dragged out of bed and pulled backwards through a hedge. Anyway, instead of standing there like a half-shut knife in that disreputable old dressing gown, for heaven's sake sit down and pay some attention to what I have to say."

"Mum, can't we get this over as quickly as possible, whatever it is you want to say to me. Thing is, I'm dead tired, had a bad, very disturbed night and I want to get back to bed. That is," with a note of sarcasm in her voice, "... if it's all right with you?"

Her mother frowned. "Actually, it's very far from all right with me as you so very naively put it. We've had you checked out by our own GP, he said by January you should be fighting fit again, no harm done from that fall you had. And since for the time being at least you still don't have a job, but are again back in the family home, you might at least try to make yourself useful. If I can go out to work on a winter's morning, nothing to prevent you from doing a spot of household shopping, a bit of dusting, even the odd bit of cooking, that sort of thing, while you're waiting to get back to some paid employment. And if you're desperate to get back to Majorca, why not re-apply as they suggested?"

Kay looked at her mother and after a moment's hesitation said: "Actually I did phone their offices the other day when you were over at Aunt Elsie's. I asked them to send me an application form to be considered for the new season, but they said they had already filled all the vacant places. Truth is, they don't want me back in that hotel, or in any other of their hotels in any one of their holiday complexes, But you still don't get it, do you?"

Her mother frowned. "Since you ask, what I don't get is this ... what exactly happened out there, that mysterious accident, how did you fall, did you fall off a donkey, fall down drunk, what? And what about the ultimate idea of becoming an airhostess?"

"Mum, I do wish you'd listen to me sometimes. I did tell you, right from day one, my eyesight let me down on that one; my legs, voice, deportment, manner, all absolutely fine, but not so my eyesight."

Her mother sighed. "In that case, if your days as a world traveller in the sun are over, then for heaven's sake bin those ridiculous hot-pants you insist on wearing. That is on the days you do get dressed at all. Get yourself into some decent clothing and by that I do not mean a coffee-stained dressing gown and a pair of ancient flip-flops or fit-for-the-bin, down at heel slippers."

Choosing to ignore the latter part of this harangue, Kay instead homed in on the subject of her prized silver lamé hotpants. "But Aunt Elsie at the airport, she said how lovely I looked in them with a gorgeous tan and my long bronzed legs."

Mrs Caxton shook her head in disbelief. "She was just being polite, poor Aunt Elsie she was as embarrassed as I was when she saw the state of you. Apart from anything else, she may just have been trying to boost your self-confidence. Fancies herself as something of an amateur phsychologist, does our Elsie now that she's in charge of a school's pastoral care programme."

The ringing of the phone from the hallway beyond cut short their conversation, but not before Kay managed to get in the last word. "Mum, that's terrible talking about your best friend like that. Honestly, these days you never have a good word to say about anybody."

As she made for the hallway, her mother turned at the door and said: "Never a good word? Well, I hope you include yourself in that list. From the state of you, I'd be hard put to find a single thing good to say about your slovenly appearance."

SIX

January gave way to an equally bleak February and for the first time ever since her earliest teen dating years, Kay much to her chagrin and utter amazement, received not a single Valentine card. Slouching around the house, going on and on about the lack of mail and the fact that nobody loved her, Kay somehow seemed to be actually luxuriating, at the same time as wallowing, in her own misery.

Launching yet again into her tale of woe, she stopped short when her mother said: "All right, so we've established, nobody loves you. Well, is it any wonder; have you looked in a mirror recently? Have you made a single positive effort either to meet up with your old friends in this neighbourhood, attempted to socialise, join something, anything?"

Kay glared at her mother, then almost as a mark of defiance, she slouched even further down into the cushions of the settee.

"I threw out my hotpants. God knows you harped on about them long enough. So they went in the dustbin, what more do you want of me? And as for your brilliant idea of my seeing and catching up with Dave, Gary, Bettina or even the Prof and his wife, you can forget all that, Mother. As of now, I have nothing in common with any single one of them."

Her mother laid down her brief case, shrugged off her trench coat and said: "That's a great pity for I've already invited Bettina round for tea tonight. I bumped into her the other day and she was delighted to be asked to come and have a meal with us. Actually, I was keeping her visit as a surprise for you, thought it might give you a bit of a lift to see an old friend."

This was greeted in silence, then, as an unwelcome truth dawned on her, Mrs Caxton asked in even tones, "Talking of food, I presume you did make the sausage stew I ordered before I left for school this morning?"

At these words, Kay lifted a cushion and holding it to her bosom, as if clinging on to a lifebelt, she looked up, appeared to summon her last reserves of energy and with the light of battle in her eyes, she snapped: "Put it this way, try this for size ... you invited her, so how about you making the damned sausage stew? And if all else fails, there's some stale cheese in the fridge. Doubtless you could work your marvellous culinary skills to create some delicious, mouth watering dish."

Mrs Caxton gasped with amazement at the utter audacity of her daughter in thus addressing her.

"Kay, I know we've had many an argument, usually over little or nothing, somehow we all too often rub each other the wrong way. But I must say, I do find it rather hard to take when out of the goodness of my heart, I try to arrange a little surprise visit from your erstwhile best friend, and then you treat me like this, it is really very hurtful."

Kay shrugged her shoulders. "Can't say that I asked you to do me any favours. Isn't it time, you let me lead my own life, free of your bloody interfering? If I should wish to see Bettina or any others of that miserable lot, then surely to heaven I'm old enough and wise enough to arrange things myself."

Grabbing up her brief case and her coat from where they still lay on the armchair, she threw her daughter a look such as one might bestow on a sworn enemy, then marched out of the room, banging the door shut behind her.

SEVEN

With the promise of Spring in the air and the approach of her twentieth birthday, Kay was already hoping that true to their long established family tradition, her beloved Dad would move heaven and earth to arrange his shore leave in order to be on hand for his daughter's annual big day. It was something of a standing family joke that Kay, more than anyone else, put such store by her birthdays. Too often her Dad would have to set sail on Christmas Eve, but Kay's birthday was sacrosanct.

As Kay sat up in bed she thought, *My birthday now, at least that's one bright spot on the horizon. But apart from that, what in God's name is the matter with me? These days far from being the star of the show, as I once was at the Faculty of Medicine, then as a children's holiday rep in Majorca, these days I can't even hold down the meanest job as a temp in any grotty junior typing pool. Never mind, come next week, Dad should be home on leave, and I'm going to make sure he's really proud of me on my birthday.*

Now that her Dad was indeed home again, and the big day had come at last, Kay awoke to the sound of her parents having a real humdinger of a row. And no matter how she strained to listen, catching only a few disjointed words, nevertheless she soon got the gist of the dispute.

I suppose Mum's beating that old drum again, yes I can hear her.

"Jim, I've said it before but I'll say it again, how is it that you can always, but always, wangle a leave for your beloved daughter's birthday ... but my birthday or even our wedding anniversary, neither one of those ever gets a mention, now does it?"

Kay smiled, mentally hugging herself as she recalled many an overheard marital row. Then reason prevailed and she thought: *All true enough what she says, poor soul, I suppose one way and another it can't be all that much fun for poor old Mum. She works hard at that school, is left in charge of me, and Dad can't even make any special efforts for her birthday.*

Another burst of shouting issued from the lounge.

But why should I bother about Mum? What about my dear old Dad, he's made a special effort to get home for me and instead of Mum being grateful and happy about that, the poor man is getting nothing but grief. Well, I can do better, I'll soon show him who in this family really appreciates his efforts to bring me happiness. I'll really please him and who knows, I might even get some Brownie points from Mum for endeavour.

She giggled like a child and for once had no problem in getting out of bed. An hour or so later, having riffled through the wardrobe, the bedroom cupboard and dressing table drawers and having left mountains of abandoned clothing scattered here, there and everywhere, Kay was feeling mightily pleased with herself. Not only had she finally located the very dress for which she had been so frantically hunting, she had discovered something else of the greatest importance.

With a spot of judicious pulling and tugging, wonder of wonder, she had finally managed to squeeze her twenty-year-old body into the floral, multi-layered confection of a party dress which she had worn for her first teenage birthday party. Not only was it the most beautiful dress she had ever possessed but it was even more special in that her Dad had bought it for her all those years ago in an upmarket store in America, With her long hair still unwashed, but now done up in an elaborate film star style, atop which backcombed mountain, she had somehow fixed an enormous chocolate-box satin ribbon. With pancake make-up, rouge, mascara and scarlet lipstick rather inexpertly applied, she sailed in full regalia into the lounge. Knowing how proud her Dad had been of her on her thirteenth birthday, she was supremely confident that one look at her carefully-won, resurrected party image would at once put paid to her parents' noisy, bitter row.

It did. In the sudden stunned silence which greeted her dramatic, highly theatrical entrance, one horrified look at her, first of all by her Mother, then by her father immediately had the desired effect. Finally, it was left to her Mother to voice their thoughts.

"Good heavens above, Kay, what next? Surely not Hallowe'en this early in the year? Having got rid of the silver lamé hot pants, I thought we'd put an end to any such ridiculous style of dressing. Honestly, here we go again and though I hate to say it, your behaviour and your dress sense is becoming more and more bizarre with every day that passes."

Ignoring her still ranting mother and glancing over at her Dad, Kay caught a strange look in his eyes, somewhere between mild amusement, bewilderment and a genuine concern for her wellbeing.

Aloud he said: "What's all this, Kay? You're not a little thirteen-year-old now, you know. Anyway ..." here he tried to inject a measure of jollity into his voice, "until I heard your Mum say that the hotpants had been dumped, I rather thought that was your preferred style of fancy dress."

At these words completely unlike what she had imagined her dear Dad would say, Kay started to tremble uncontrollably. Then she broke down in an avalanche of tears.

"But, Dad, I thought, I was sure you'd be so proud of me, you used to like to see me in this party dress."

For once in his life ignoring this heartbroken plea for parental approval, he went across and just held Kay in his arms in silence, all the while letting her cry her bitter tears.

Then over the top of her head, he whispered: "For heaven's sake, Janet, how long has she been behaving like this? If you ask me, more than high time you frogmarched her along to a doctor."

Kay looked up through her tears, the river of which had already created havoc with the overheavy make-up. Like a waif or a broken doll, she peered up at her Dad and for once she took her mother's side. "Dad, please don't blame Mum, it isn't her fault. Listen, I've already been to see our GP on my own. I never said a word to Mum."

Mrs Caxton leapt in, in horrified tones. "Dear God, so now you've been to see the doctor in secret. Don't, please, do not tell me you're pregnant? Is that what this charade has been about?"

Her Dad frowned. "Kay, what precisely did Doctor Graham say? I know he checked you out not long after your accident when you first came home, Mum accompanied you on that occasion and she told me you'd got a clean bill of health.. But what exactly did he say to you on your latest visit?"

Kay cleared her throat. "He said I'd be fine, just fine, certainly a bit below par, not unsurprising given the fact of my now being unemployed, having lost touch with all my friends, and now being away from the lovely lifestyle I'd clearly enjoyed in the Majorcan sunshine."

Again her father frowned. "And that was it? That was all he said, didn't suggest any treatment, or medication of any kind?"

Kay looked down at her feet and stared hard at her gold party shoes with the little bows along the front.

"Kay, I've asked you a direct question for which I would like an answer."

Kay looked up in surprise at the strict tone of voice so unusual from her Dad, and after clearing her throat a couple of times she said: "He did tell me to stop worrying about everything and nothing. To try to get as much rest as possible and ... he gave me pills to take, three a day in the morning and another two at bedtime."

Mrs Caxton shook her head. "I knew nothing about any pills."

The Captain shot his wife a look. "Pills, what exactly are these pills for, what precisely was the doctor's diagnosis? After all, no doctor worthy of the name would simply hand out pills like sweeties without having some idea of what he was supposed to be treating. I repeat, what are the pills for?"

Her mother broke in. "As usual, it's all down to me, all my fault. I didn't know she was taking medication of any kind and ..."

Her father waved aside her mother's words. "Janet, for once this is not about you. It may have escaped your notice but I am very seriously concerned. Katherine, for the last time, what precise name did Doctor Graham give to your condition? I am, of course, assuming that your mother's rather hasty diagnosis of an unwanted or unplanned pregnancy is utterly wrong. What did he say the pills were for?"

On hearing her beloved father using her Sunday name as opposed to the more casual endearing term of Kay, she again broke down in a paroxysm of weeping. When at last she had recovered sufficiently to speak coherently, she said: "Depression, that's what he said, a mild case of depression, winter blues. He said I am depressed."

A look of horror on her Dad's face stopped any further discussion and it was left to her Mother to say: "Depressed indeed! If anybody knows about that condition, it should be me. Post-natal depression, I've suffered from that for close on twenty years now, ever since the very date and day you were born, my girl."

Her husband got to his feet. "Janet, that is more than enough and your own self-pitying whine isn't going to help any one of us in this situation. I suggest you get our daughter cleaned up, help her into bed, while I phone for the doctor, seems to me it's rather more than a mild attack of depression. I'm no doctor but we need help and we need it now."

At the mention of a visit from the doctor, Kay protested: "No, Dad, I don't need the doctor, just let me rest and I'll be fine. I'll keep taking the pills, I'm sure they're helping me."

"With regard to the bloody pills, I daresay they have side effects and they can't possibly be doing you any kind of good."

Janet spoke up. "Actually, Jim, apart from this morning's episode, she has been a little better of late, so couldn't we hold off about specialists for the moment. Let her have a good rest and then after a week or so, see how things are shaping up?"

Jim turned to his wife. "Janet, you and I need to talk calmly, rationally about this. So please get Kay settled in bed for a rest, then we'll discuss the matter in private."

Ignoring her husband's order to get Kay into bed, instead Janet Caxton looked at her husband in amazement.

"I just don't believe this. Here you are, you breeze in from the high seas, criticise your beloved daughter's dress sense and on the strength of that, you decide in your wisdom that she's mentally ill."

Jim put out a hand as if to sweep aside her words. "For heaven's sake, That's an over-simplification of facts and ..."

Janet got to her feet. "For God's sake, spare me the Captain's report and the amateur psychology. Honestly, Jim when you look around these days, most people seem as if they'd got dressed in the dark. But you don't bung all and sundry into a mental hospital because their dress-code offends you, now do you?"

He gave a snort of anger. "That's ridiculous, you're talking nonsense, anyway, you yourself said about how difficult and decidedly bizarre her behaviour has been for ages now."

Janet raised her eyes to heaven. "That's true enough, but from my experience all teenagers are downright difficult, bloody-minded in fact not to put too fine a point on it. So if a teenager's hormones are running riot, I tend to the view that it's something their long suffering parents just have to deal with until they grow out of it."

He shook his head. "Difficult behaviour and downright cussedness is one thing, but when it comes to someone of her age dressing up like some sort of latter-day Shirley Temple, that's an entirely different matter. That's my thinking on the matter. That's why I believe we should be getting in some specialist help before we get into deeper waters."

As their argument got more and more heated, suddenly Janet realised that at some point in the noisy slanging match, Kay had crept off quietly to bed. Pointing this out to her husband, Janet said: "Of the three of us, Kay's the only sensible one, if you ask me, at least she knows when to shut up and go off back to bed for a rest and get the hell out of this screaming row."

He glowered at Janet. "Sit down; we must discuss this more calmly, in a more rational manner. This is solving nothing and it is imperative that something be done. If Kay's recent behaviour is what passes for normal teenage behaviour, than all I can say is, it's a wonder they ever survive to mature into perfectly sane adults."

Perching on the edge of the nearest chair, Janet said: "Jim, you can decide all you want, but there is one point which you've conveniently overlooked. Kay has been sufficiently responsible in her own right, in that she has already seen our own doctor. Don't forget she did that off her own bat, not a word about any such appointment to me, surely that was a reasonably adult way for her to go about it? So can't we at least leave matters as they are for the moment; see how that works out, before we go stirring things up with mental illness specialists and the like?"

Jim pursed his lips. "I believe they're called psychiatrists." Having corrected her on the precise nomenclature, he sat in silence for several moments. Then as if having reached a decision, his face cleared. "Perhaps rest, a period of greater calm, especially as you're so determined that her behaviour is more or less normal in a teenager. Listen, let's try it, if you can stand it, so I suppose, must I.

But one thing I will do, first thing tomorrow I'll pop into town, something I want to do." Janet glared at him. "Here we go. As usual, I suppose you're hell-bent on spoiling Kay. Some expensive gift from Rackhams? A new charm bracelet, Daddy will make it better?"

He glared at her. "Actually it was rather more the Bull Ring, I had in mind."

It was nearly lunchtime next day before her husband arrived back from his avowed mission to the city centre. But for once, far from being festooned with parcels and expensive-looking carrier bags from all the best stores, he was empty-handed. On entering the lounge, he looked around the room expectantly.

"Kay gone out for a walk, has she?"

Janet gave a tut of exasperation. "Well seen, you're hardly ever home from roaming the mighty oceans of the world, otherwise you'd know, Kay seldom gets out of bed at all these days, far less venture outside. A walk indeed."

He waved her to a seat and at once said: "Now, Janet, I am not about to have yet another row with you. But one thing I really must say, the way you tell it, anyone would think that I go to sea for my own enjoyment. For God's sake, woman, it's my career, my occupation and I might add, our bread and butter."

Janet frowned. "It seems to have escaped your notice that I too work, I too have a career, and I work damned hard to help maintain our privileged lifestyle."

He sighed. "Like I say, no more rows, please. Why not, for once just listen to what I've been up to in town this morning. I've only gone and booked a holiday. There now, and what do you think of that?"

It was the last thing Janet had expected and she could only repeat: "A holiday?"

He nodded, smiling. "Don't tell me I've actually done something right for once, something that pleases you?"

Janet waited for him to go on. "Yes, a change of scenery, a bit of sea air, do Kay a world of good. She's never been to Torquay before. Be a really nice change for her."

Janet took a step back. "Torquay? Why there of all places?"

He grinned. "Why not? After all it was good enough for our honeymoon. Any way, when I went to the travel agents, they had on their list a short coach tour, leaves on Monday morning and last minute or not, I managed to get the very last available seats."

Janet could feel a weight lifting from her shoulders at the thought of a half-term away from the city. "Oh that's marvellous, Jim, and how very lucky to get the last seats. That will do us all good, a short break, just what the doctor would have ordered."

He gave a rather nervous, apologetic cough. "Actually, thing is, it isn't for all of us, there were only two seats and one double room left on the coach tour." She let this information sink in. "You don't mean to tell me, you're packing me off with Kay, while you stay here luxuriating in the peace and quiet of having the bungalow to yourself?"

He gave her a studied look. "Not quite the way I'd have put it. So much for my good deed and my bright idea."

She got to her feet "Good deed, be damned. Honestly, Jim how could you have been so stupid? Surely even you must have noticed over time, left to ourselves. Kay and I are like two bulldogs in a bathtub. Hadn't thought of that aspect of the mother-daughter relationship now had you?"

His face like thunder, he said: "Well, warring partners or not, it's all arranged and paid for now, so like it or lump it, come Monday morning, the pair of you are off on a coach tour."

Janet clenched and unclenched her hands. "I'm getting a bad feeling about this and, no, to hell with it all. I've made up my mind, I'm not going."

Just then Kay slippered her way into the room and at once her Dad said: "Hello there, darling. Had a nice rest have you? Anyway, there's good news, I've booked a little holiday for you and your Mum, you'd like that, wouldn't you?"

Janet knew that had Jim not breenged in and told Kay about the proposed holiday before the matter had been fully discussed, then without a doubt she would have dug in her heels and refused to go on any such junket. However, having once seen in her daughter's eyes the most animation she'd seen in months, she knew, she would, of necessity, have to go along.

When Monday morning came, an over-jovial Captain Jim leapt out of bed at the first ping of the alarm clock and shook Janet by the shoulder.

"Rising bell, rise and shine, old girl, rise and shine."

A Daughter is for Life

Knowing herself to be at less than her best and grumpy with it, at five o'clock on a half-term morning, Janet mumbled something uncomplimentary into her pillow and then snuggled further down under the blankets and the eiderdown.

When he again shook her, she said: "You do know it's half-term, so just bugger off. Why would I want to get up at this ungodly hour? If you want to rouse somebody, why not try your luck with Kay? And jolly good luck with that, for these days, she tends to stick to her bed these days like chewing gum to a hairy blanket."

He answered: "A sizzling bacon-butty should do the trick with Kay, especially when I remind her about the holiday starting today. She'll not want to miss out on that. You said yourself how very enthusiastic she seemed."

Janet sat up in bed and pushing a lock of hair out of her eyes gasped: "Oh, God, the holiday, I'd forgotten all about that."

Some hour and a half later Jim, still in good spirits at having achieved the virtually impossible in getting his crew organised and in good time, got them safely to the coach station. On the point of Jim giving his wife and daughter a farewell embrace, Kay suddenly backed away. "Why are you saying goodbye, Dad, I thought this was to be a family holiday?"

Janet and her husband exchanged glances and it was on the tip of Janet's tongue to say: "Told you so, didn't I?" but then she thought, *All right you made the arrangement, let's see how you get out of this.*

As Jim started to explain to Kay the mechanics of the late booking, Kay's eyes filled with tears.

"You're not coming because you don't love me. You didn't like my party dress and now you don't like me." He held out a hand to placate her, but by now weeping noisily, Kay would have none of it.

As they made their way to their allotted seats, Kay was still weeping and muttering: "Still don't see why he can't come, this is all your doing, you want me all for yourself."

As her husband's face faded from view, Janet could not banish the thought: *All right for him, that's his parental duty done. As per usual, I'm the one left with the hard part.*

Once settled in their seats, Janet swivelled her head and took stock of her fellow passengers, not a full head of hair to be seen on the men and the women as if having come off some sort of hairdressers assembly line, they all sported grey, white or blue-rinsed hair styled in tight little 'Brillopad' over-permed concoctions.

Not a pony-tail in sight to chum up with Kay, and certainly not anyone suitable in my age-range either. It's going to be one hell of a holiday this, not exactly a knees-up. Talk about God's waiting room on wheels. No sooner had Janet thought this than she mentally reprimanded herself. Be old myself one day, that's to say if I manage to survive the trauma of parenthood.

She cast a sideways glance at her daughter who apparently less than interested in the people around her or their hairstyles, far less the passing scene from her window-seat, was instead doing up the many buttons on the jacket of her trouser-suit. Then, having studiously checked that each and every button was securely fastened, she then went on to unbutton each in turn before starting the entire process all over again.

Janet could feel her heart sink to the bottom of her stomach as she watched this mindless performance. In a bid to divert Kay from such intense concentration on the self-appointed futile exercise, Janet leant towards her proffering a bag of Woolworth's pick-n-mix. Kay took one look at the open bag of goodies, frowned and then recoiled as if in abject terror of some very real and imminent danger. In voice hoarse with stark fear, she said: "No, I won't take all those pills, you can't make me, no, you're not my doctor."

Janet put a hand to her mouth to stifle at birth the scream of panic she could feel rising to her lips. Then with a supreme effort of willpower, taking a firm grip on her own turmoil of emotions, she whispered: "It's all right, dear, it's sweets in the bag, sweets not pills. Look, I'll take one. Sure you don't want to join me?"

Kay rebuttoned her jacket. "You can take all the pills you want, but you can't catch me out that way. You'll not drug me. He hates us doesn't he? I suppose he told you to get rid of me with pills. But no, I will not take them. You can't make me."

Janet feeling sick to her stomach – not even a modicum of comfort – she hasn't once addressed me as Mum or even the often rather frosty Mother when she is seriously upset.

She leant closer to her daughter and whispered: "Sh, now dear we don't want to disturb the other passengers now do we? And if you really don't want any dolly mixtures, or jelly babies, then I'll put them back into my handbag, no problem whatsoever. Perhaps you'd like a magazine to riffle through; I popped a couple in my bag at the last moment, in case we get bored on the journey."

Kay lifted her head, stared hard at her mother and in a voice such as one would use when addressing an intrusive and not particularly bright stranger, and said: "It may have escaped your notice, Madam, but I am already rather engaged. This jacket and its fastenings require my urgent attention. So thanks but no thank you, I want neither magazine, drugs of any kind nor even your bloody interference every five minutes."

Then raising her voice and in a crystal-clear voice which caused heads to turn she yelled: "What part of the word No is it that you do not understand? I said no and I mean no. Just bloody well give it a rest and leave me alone ... ALONE ... alone, do you get the message?"

By now fully aware that most people on the bus had heard the message loud and clear, Janet closed her eyes, feigned sleep and turned her thoughts inwards to the chaos now surging through her brain.

A short holiday? Is that what you called it, Jim? I rather think this is going to be the longest few days of my entire life. God help me. God help both of us, for already I think we're in rather dire straits. What in God's name will be the outcome of all this? And by now, I'd guess our fellow passengers are wondering the very same thing, certainly something to write about on their holiday postcards home: 'Having a terrible time, glad you're not here. Talk about neighbours from hell, try fellow passengers from hell.'

It seemed they had hardly started on the journey when the coach driver announced over the tannoy, "Ladies and gentleman, we shall be making the first of our comfort stops at the Cosy Corner Cafe in about fifteen minutes time. As well as tea and coffee there is also a gift shop and with half an hour's leisure, you can enjoy browsing and have a bit of what I believe you ladies refer to as retail therapy. That suit everybody?"

A smattering of applause and polite laughter at the corny joke, all of which was marred only by Kay's comment: "A comfort stop. For God's sake, Mother, does he think we're all geriatrics, all hooked on water pills? Will that suit everybody? Hmph, it bloody well doesn't suit me."

Those in the near vicinity, on overhearing this acerbic comment, craned their heads round and gave Kay and her mother meaningful looks. Janet pulled her daughter closer to her side. "Sh now, dear, just relax. A nice cuppa and browsing for knickknacks, we'll both enjoy that, won't we? It'll break the tedium of the journey."

Kay gave a hoarse laugh. "I might enjoy it if I happened to be in my dotage like this busload of decrepit wrecks."

Janet tightened her hold on her daughter's arm. "Kay, that really is enough. I won't hear another word."

Kay jerked her arm free. "Oh, sorry, but you'll be in line to hear plenty more words from me, Don't forget, we're stuck together on this bloody coach. A holiday? Is that your name for it?"

When the coach drew up at the Cosy Corner Cafe the passengers started to alight, despite walking sticks at the ready, moving rather slowly and painfully. Kay tapped her foot in impatience. When a rush from the back of the queue from the more agile passengers caused a sort of bottleneck at the exit Kay suddenly said in an overloud voice. "At this rate, Mother, the comfort stop will be rather too late in coming. Those water pills are known to have a sort of time limit and it seems some folk are getting pretty desperate."

Gasps, muttered comments and downright dirty looks were the end result of this latest tirade. And by the time they were in the business of looking for a table, most seats had been taken or were already booked with jackets and coat.

EIGHT

"Right from the word go, the holiday was an unmitigated disaster," Janet said to her waiting husband as she alighted from the bus at the coach-station.

As she ushered Kay towards her Dad, her daughter's face wore a puzzled frown. "Who's that come to meet us?"

At that one sentence, Janet felt the bottom fall out of her world. She turned to face Kay with the words: "Kay for heaven's sake I know you're tired after the journey and we're both really upset after that terrible carry-on in the bus, but do please at least summon a smile for your Dad."

As Jim stepped forward, clearly about to embrace his daughter, she recoiled in horror and screamed: "Get away from me. Who are you? Get away, don't touch me."

Other fellow passengers from their bus hurried past with eyes downcast and heads bent. Already sufficiently annoyed at the trauma, delay and general inconvenience on their homeward journey when Kay had had to be physically restrained by her mother from jumping off the moving coach in the middle of the motorway, they clearly wanted no further involvement in whatever ongoing family drama was then being played out. Despite his normal seafaring tan Jim looked ashen as he stared in horror at his daughter.

Janet felt they were all three of them stuck fast in some hideous time-warp, from which they would never emerge. And as if watching actors in a melodrama, the thought crazy as it was, raced through Janet's brain: "Percival paled beneath his manly tan."

Then as one wakening from a nightmare, Jim turned to his wife with the words: "What did you say? Have you lost your wits as well? Quick, the car's parked over there. Help me get Kay into the car, then you sit in the back seat with her." As he again approached his beloved daughter, Kay like a terrified animal caught in a trap, tried to back away, no longer screaming but moaning and keening. Even more pitiful and heart-rending was her pathetic mantra: "Don't want you, I want my Daddy, I want my Daddy, Daddy, help."

Safely back home with Kay still under the impression that her Dad was a stranger, she had allowed her Mum to tuck her up in bed and now appeared to be sleeping soundly. Janet tiptoed from the room and went into the lounge where her husband was waiting with a mug of coffee for each of them.

As Janet sipped at hers, she mused: "I believe a good strong drink might have been more appropriate."

Jim nodded. "I agree, but for the moment, I think we both must keep a clear head. From what I've seen today and from even the sketchiest details you've so far given me of the holiday ... I must say from attempted suicide in jumping off a moving coach on the motorway, disparaging comments about the other passengers from the word go, and her totally bizarre behaviour at mealtimes ... it all sounds horrendous and..."

Janet bent forward. "No need to remind me, Jim, don't forget I lived the nightmare. Honestly I've had more pleasant nightmares. Anyway, she's your daughter too, so let's hear what your master plan is now. For the love of heaven, please do not suggest another holiday, that would finish me altogether."

He gave her a sour look. "Don't know that it would do Kay all that much good either. Anyway, we're not about to get into any more slanging matches, so perhaps a small libation of something stronger than coffee, might calm us both down a bit. Then we'll discuss what's to be done. And remember, I'm as much in the dark as you. Never had to deal with a situation like this before, now have we?"

Janet gave a rueful smile. "I thought that baby teething troubles and teenage mood swings were as bad as it could get."

Jim took a long drink of his whisky. "From what I've witnessed today, I do think we need specialist help and we need it as like yesterday. A bout of mild depression is one thing, but I think we're dealing with something a lot more serious. I'd hesitate to put a name to it."

Janet said: "I'm no doctor nor are you, but I think we can forget depression. I don't suppose you've thought of schizophrenia; now there's a name and condition to conjure with."

"Janet. That's more than enough; it's our daughter we're talking about. There's not another minute to spare, I'm due back on my ship next week and I want this matter dealt with now."

On the first of several house-calls, Dr Graham confirmed his earlier diagnosis as previously given to Kay herself, Now, in meeting with Janet and her husband, he finished with the throwaway comment: "And let us not forget , such a sudden and dramatic change in Kay's life, that would depress the stoutest spirit." He then went on to suggest the name of an excellent psychiatrist of high repute who, if and when required, could be consulted privately. Having said that he then frowned "Come to think of it, there might just be one small problem. As I say, Mr Swanwick is the very best in his field, but to the best of my knowledge, he is currently away on a lecture tour abroad, promoting his latest book on juvenile mental illness."

The stark reality of the words mental illness hung in the air like an avenging force of evil.

Jim looked down at his daughter where she sat on the settee, as if waiting orders as to where she should now be going, what she should now be doing. Terrified that the cruel label of mental illness had pierced and already invaded her mind, he again looked hard at her. But she appeared at that moment to be in a world of her own as she sat busily plaiting the long fringes of the poncho which she wore on her shoulders.

Having heard Dr. Graham's opinion, Jim said: "Thank you for your help, Doctor and in view of what you've told me, I'll make arrangements for additional shore leave until such time as we can get to see your Mister Swanwick. Yes, I do believe that would be the best thing to do, after all, Kay just loves it when her Dad's home from sea."

Dr Graham looked down at his patient, then patting her kindly on the head said: "Mm, Actually, Captain, no real need for that. It may take several weeks until Mister Swanwick returns from abroad. Meantime, since I gather that you, Mrs Caxton, can get leave of absence from your school, and if you're prepared to weather the storm until then, I do think it would be best to make as few changes in the home routine as possible. And of course, I'll be keeping an eye on the situation with house-calls. You think you'd be happy with that arrangement, Mrs Caxton?"

Janet shrugged her shoulders. "I don't know that happy is quite the word I'd use, but if this is the way forward to help Kay, then yes, of course, I'll go along with what you say."

Jim started to protest. "I honestly think my wife has had enough trauma. For heaven's sake, surely this Mister Swanwick isn't the only specialist in the field, there must be somebody else we can get in touch with immediately?"

"You're right, of course, Captain, but Swanwick is the very best in his field. Put it this way, I have three daughters and if this had happened to any one of them, then however long it might take, I'd be prepared to weather the storm with a GP's help until such time as we could consult the top man. There, does that answer your question?"

Looking less than convinced, Jim started again to protest. "Even so, I do think I should cancel my next trip, be here for Kay and her Mum."

The doctor waved aside his words. "Let's not forget the old adage: Two's company, three's a crowd. It's best to keep everything as normal and as near to the usual family routine as possible ... at least until circumstances dictate otherwise. You'll have my full cooperation. So are we agreed?"

As the doctor said his goodbyes, suddenly Kay abandoned her industrious plaiting, looked up and said: "I'm in charge of cooking tonight, Mum told me to make a sausage stew, so I'd better get busy. You'll stay for tea, won't you, you'll like Bettina, Mum's invited her too. I hope you all like my special sausage stew, make a change from fish fingers, won't it?"

NINE

Some two weeks later, Kay, having enjoyed being well and truly spoiled by her Mum's undivided attention, and with pleasant visits from Bettina who brought news from the outside world, was feeling more relaxed than she'd felt in many a long day. This was especially so when on each of Bettina's visits, the latter said: "You'll soon be up and about again, I don't suppose that tummy bug you picked up on holiday can last forever. Anyway I'll phone your Mum on Sunday and hopefully pop in again next week."

Quite happily sitting up in bed with an unopened magazine on her lap, Kay was surprised when one afternoon Doctor Graham arrived with another gentleman in tow. The well-dressed stranger's examination, if indeed that's what it was meant to be, was brief and consisted of little more than a sort of free-and-easy bedside chat, after which he stalked out of the room and stood talking to her Mum in the hallway beyond. By now something of an expert in the art of eavesdropping, Kay made out enough of the conversation to learn that the following day a new plan was afoot. Her mother was to take her along to some hospital or other where the man had consulting rooms and there he would examine the patient in greater detail.

The patient! Hmph, I suppose by that he means me. Bloody cheek, nothing wrong with me. Still if it gets me out of the house for a few hours, I might even meet up with some of the Dr Kildare types from the Faculty of Medicine, so why not, play along with it all?

The matter thus settled in her own mind, mentally Kay was already planning her outfit for her big day out. Her last waking thought before she drifted off to the pill-induced sleep was: Pity Mum made me throw out my lovely silver lamé pants. Those yummy medical students and young doctors, they would have loved seeing me in my gorgeous hot-pants. And even though my tan has long since faded, I do still have the legs to carry them off. Roll on tomorrow, a day of freedom. I'm really looking forward to it. After a quick visit to the hospital, I'll persuade Mum to go into town with me, a bit of shopping and a nice lunch, what could be better?

Early next morning, to Janet's surprise, Kay needed no prolonged coaxing to get her out of bed. A cat's lick with a dampened face flannel, a flurry of talcum powder over her body and a liberal dusting of the same brushed through her hair, and Kay felt good as new. Once dressed and on the point of applying a dash of lipstick, she suddenly thought the better of this, as she recalled a dim memory, something about the fact of her Dad's not liking her to sport make-up of any kind. As Kay and her mother left the house and into the waiting taxi, on catching sight of the local postman, Kay gave him a cheery wave. Then turning to her mother, she gave a high-pitched laugh together with the words: "I expect that's my usual pile of fan mail. For a while, it seemed as if nobody loved me any more, but now, hardly a day goes by but what there's a stack of valentines for me in the post. Great that, isn't it?"

Still in the rosy glow of her high hopes for a pleasant day out, a quick chat with the kindly Mr Swanwicksong, or whatever his name was, and then a spot of lunch at their favourite restaurant in town, after which hopefully, she could break free of her Mum and head in glorious freedom for an afternoon of extravagant spend, spend, spending funded by the money her Dad had left for a rainy day.

Not raining of course, Kay smiled to herself. But I'm sure Dad will be happy to see my new wardrobe of stylish clothes, but not party frocks, I seem to remember, he no longer likes to see me in a frilly party dress. So, something more elegant and, of course, hugely expensive from Rackhams, that's the idea.

As they got out of the taxi at the entrance to the hospital, Kay grinned. "Right Mum, a quick chat, then we're out of here. What do you fancy for lunch today? I'm fed up with fish fingers and sausage stew, think I'll go mad and have nice expensive scampi and then ..."

As Kay turned to face her Mother, she was surprised to see tears pouring down her Mother's cheeks.

Kay stamped her foot angrily on the pavement. "Oh, well, if you begrudge me a decent meal all that much, I suppose I'll have to settle for something cheaper, how about macaroni cheese, that all right?"

Janet patted her daughter's arm. "No need to get yourself upset, dear, if it's scampi you really want, then honestly no problem, we'll spare no expense."

As Janet Caxton escorted her beloved daughter, her yet again happily chattering, grinning only child into the hospital on that beautiful spring morning, she knew that it was the single most difficult thing she had ever had to do in her entire life. Gulping down her tears of bitter anguish, she wondered if she had been less than honest with Kay?

Should she, indeed could she, possibly have put the matter more plainly to her, instead of leaving so much unsaid? But on the other hand and even though she was obeying the Consultant's advice to the letter, she argued with herself, "How in God's name could I ever summon the courage, the inner strength or even the guts to say, "Listen, Kay, dear, sorry about this, but from what the doctors say, it seems there is a strong possibility ... rather more of a foregone conclusion ... that as of now you are to be labelled mentally ill. And while we're at it, I might as well be totally honest , spill the beans, and let you know that this is no ordinary hospital we're entering."

Thus ran Janet's tortured thoughts as they were ushered into the designated consulting room and where already seated at a massive oak desk were two doctors in the company of Mr Swanwick. From the brevity of the interview which followed, something was at once abundantly clear to Janet. She knew with an inner gut feeling. This meeting, this charade is merely a formality. They have already decided on a firm diagnosis and even a label for my darling Kay's condition. This performance in which I too as her next-of-kin must play my part, this is a legal formality which must by law be strictly observed before my wee girl can be admitted for treatment.

Janet emerged from the inner torment of dark thoughts to the realisation that somehow or other the next stage in the ordered proceedings had been reached.

When it came to the point of two hefty male attendants, presumably nursing orderlies, entering the room with the clear purpose of escorting Kay elsewhere in the hospital, then, in stark contrast to the previous controlled calm of proceedings, all hell broke loose. As she seemed suddenly to realise what was happening, Kay let out a blood curdling scream, a sound which cut straight into Janet's heart and soul; a shriek which she would remember until her dying day. With the look of a trapped animal which had been cruelly tricked into such a dire situation, Kay turned and shot her mother a venomous look.

"Look, Mum, we were getting on so well, beginning to understand each other. Why have you done this to me? You promised me a lunch in town, some luxury shopping, a big spending spree, I just don't understand it. Oh, to hell with it, I hate you. I want my Daddy. I want my Daddy. He would never treat me like this, have me dragged into this nut house."

With what inner strength she had left, Janet said: "Kay, darling, honestly, it's for your own good, you are ill and if the doctors say you have to be sectioned to ..."

Another heart rending shriek. "God, Daddy, somebody, please help me. Section me, so now you're going to let them cut me up into bits, why Mum, why? I don't want to be sectioned, don't cut me up in bits"

A nod of the head from the Consultant and the two nursing orderlies forcibly marched Kay from the room. She was still screaming, shouting, yelling obscenities and curses, disgusting words such as Janet had never before heard pass her daughter's lips. Even as the cries died away, somehow the echo, real or imagined by now and the pitiful chant of "Don't section me into bits," still seemed to hang in the air. And far from its all being a hideous nightmare from which Janet would awaken at any moment, the next words addressed to her shattered any such vain pathetic hope. The Consultant, placing his elbows on the desk leant forward and having made a pyramid of his fingertips, said: "You must remember we are all experts in this field of mental illness and your daughter will be well taken care of. However, we do realise what a blow this is for you, so in the next few minutes, if you have any outstanding queries, we'll be more than happy to address them."

Janet knew she had an entire battery of questions, any single one of which would have taken hours rather than a few hurried moments to address. But where to start, what to ask first and what in God's name would be of most immediate help to her in this hour of need? Summoning all her willpower and determined not to appear the snivelling, pathetic shell of a mother which by now she inwardly knew herself to be, she squared her shoulders, cleared her throat and asked, "I imagine by now you have already put some sort of name-tag to Kay's condition?" The three medical men exchanged meaningful glances and Janet could have sworn that one of their number gave a barely imperceptible, but warning shake of the head.

Finally, the spokesman looked Janet squarely in the eyes. "Let me put it this way, Mrs Caxton, you are an intelligent woman, Dr Graham informs me that you are headmistress of that excellent, exclusive school at which his own daughters are being so well educated. However," here he looked to his colleagues for their head-nodding support, " let's leave any actual name-tags for the moment. Suffice to say, it is our considered opinion your daughter is very ill, she does need specialist help which she will get here in this hospital. Beyond that, all we are prepared to spell out, is the fact that Kay is suffering a massive personality disorder."

The younger of the three doctors nodded. "That sums it up, a personality disorder, now then that doesn't sound too earth-shattering now does it?"

Determined not to be patronised in this way, no matter how well-meaning the intention, Janet sat up straighter in her chair.

"Suppose for the moment anyway I am prepared to accept such a simplified layman's term for my daughter's illness, but now I need to know ... why does she have it, how and when exactly did it start and is there anything I could possibly have done to prevent such a thing happening to her?"

Again those shared meaningful looks, as they were silently debating just how much medical information they should impart.

Mister Swanwick said: "Current thinking in informed psychiatric circles is that ... the sudden onset of mental illness initially relates to a child's upbringing. There can, of course, be other triggers such as trauma, but it's upbringing that ..."

Janet gasped. "You mean, parents are to blame? Why I never heard anything so preposterous. Not much comfort for me then in that hare-brained theory is there. Kay had a wonderful childhood, she was always a happy, well-adjusted child; she was well-loved. And now you tell me ..."

In the silence which followed, as Janet sat clenching and unclenching her hands, the Consultant started to gather up his sheaf of papers from the desk-pad in front of him, a clear signal that the meeting was over.

As he rose to his feet and stretched over to shake her hand, he said: "Best thing I can advise for the sake of your own health, Mrs Caxton, is get back to work, keep your mind occupied, especially since there is a strict no-visiting rule for such patients at least in the first few weeks."

At these words, at a blow indicating this would be no simple overnight hospital stay for her daughter, Kay rose to go.

As she turned away, the Consultant said: "But we have your telephone number and if there is the possibility that Kay should require electro-convulsive therapy, then of course you would be called in to sign the necessary consent forms."

Her heart breaking with this latest hammer-blow, Janet got out of the consulting room before she too, like Kay, delivered herself of a scream.

TEN

A suggested reviving cup of tea in the hospital's canteen, where she was surrounded by other wan, utterly distraught almost zombie-like parents and visitors, did little to calm Janet's twanging nerves. And to make matters worse other people around her, all seemed to have a husband, wife, or a compassionate friend on hand with whom to share the horrific burden of dealing with the trauma of having a loved one as a patient in a mental hospital. In that moment of crystal-clear clarity of vision, Janet realised how utterly alone she was. Leaving the now cold dregs of the oversweet tea, she got to her feet and feeling as if walking on eggs, she stumbled her way out of the hospital.

Walking through the grounds towards the tall gates, the pleasant warmth of the spring sunshine, the sound of the birds chirping and the waving of a host of golden daffodils, all struck her senses like an actual physical blow. Even worse, the normality, the bloody uncaring, unthinking normality of everyone else in the streets going about their daily business seemed like a hideous obscenity, a deliberate assault on her already broken spirit.

Talk about kicking a woman when she's down, she thought.

Then she could feel an inner anger boiling to the surface.

Did no one else in this entire world even care in the slightest that her beloved only daughter had that very morning been, what was it they'd called it ... what was the word Kay had taken such objection to in the belief it meant they were going to cut her up into pieces ... sectioned, that was it. Yes, sectioned legally and thus committed to a psychiatric ward.

Oh, yes, she thought, *they can dress up the name of the hospital any fancy way they want and call it the something or other nerve hospital. But the reality, the nightmare is this, my darling wee girl; my bright shining star, is now languishing in a lunatic asylum. Oh, dear God help me, a lunatic asylum. How do I tell my husband that bit of news when he phones from his travels. As for the very mention of electro-convulsive therapy, God give me strength.*

Even years afterwards, Janet could never recall in the slightest detail how she had managed to make it safely home that day, nor indeed when the time arose, how she imparted the dire news to her husband. One thing she did remember, would always remember for the rest of her life with appalling mind-blowing clarity was the phone call a few days after Kay's admittance to advise Janet that her daughter had somehow managed to escape from the hospital, wearing only a nightie.

Then no sooner had Janet been informed some twenty-four hours later that Kay had been caught hiding in the hospital grounds, than Janet got yet another phone call, in response to which here she was again heading for another meeting with Kay's doctors. If Janet had thought the earlier consultation difficult, then compared to what she was now being asked to agree to, the previous meeting had been little short of a walk in the park.

She gazed in utter disbelief. "You mean that given this latest development, my daughter's mental condition is now such that this electrical treatment, it's virtually her only hope of making any sort of meaningful recovery?"

Dr Davis nodded. "I know it does sound rather extreme, but in my considerable experience with such cases it has always shown to have remarkable results."

Janet pursed her lips. "I feel ill at the very thought of such a barbaric treatment, especially when it's up to me to sign the consent form. No, I'm sorry, I won't do it, not until I've given the matter considerably more thought and at least until my husband is home from sea, in about six weeks time."

A Daughter is for Life

Dr Davis gave her a pitying look. "I know it is difficult for you, no one ever likes to give the go-ahead for ECT, but we must have a decision today, time is of the essence."

Unable to face the hospital canteen, Janet instead went into a nearby cafe for a cup of tea in the hope it would somehow control the trembling and raw emotion which threatened to engulf her. Ever since the moment she had put pen to paper, on that accursed form. Her right hand had seemed to have developed a frenetic, trembling life of its own. She had already inadvertently sloshed the best part of the cup's contents on to the plastic table in front of her when she looked up and saw Kay's friend, Bettina.

"I thought it was you I saw coming in here. Save me a phone call, my Mother wants to have you and Kay round to our place for a meal this coming Saturday, seven o'clock or thereabouts."

Janet stared up at the fresh-faced, pony-tailed young woman.

"Bettina, if you have a minute sit down, please join me in a cuppa, there's something I have to tell you."

The news was soon told, or rather an edited version which elicited the immediate response: "Oh, poor old Kay, in for tests. Never mind, she's like me, strong as a horse, soon be right as rain, Anyway, tell me the number of her ward and which hospital she's in and I'll pop round at visiting time tonight. Take her some grapes."

The moment Janet said the name of the Nerve Hospital, a strange, almost scared look came over the young woman's face. "Oh, my mistake, I took it for granted she'd be in the general hospital, that's where they treat stomach troubles, not in that other place. Come to think of it, I don't know that I am free for hospital visiting tonight after all."

Janet, with a still trembling hand, laid down her cup. "To save you the embarrassment, Bettina, it's not exactly the Victorian lunatic asylum of popular imagination, but no visitors allowed. So, no need for you to go within a mile of the Nerve Hospital. Also, I take it that the invitation for Saturday no longer stands?"

Bettina's sudden look of utter relief said it all. "Oh, sorry, I didn't mean to imply ..."

Janet nodded. "No need to apologise, Bettina. In fact, you've just proved a very valid point for me ... in all of the books I got from the library on the subject, there was some mention of the unwarranted, yet very real stigma with regard to mental illness. I rather doubted that such would be the case, but, like I say, in one short episode, you've proved the point for me ... that such stigma is indeed still alive and well and in the forefront of other people's minds with regard to mental illness."

Bettina's face went scarlet. "That's a bit unfair, Mrs Caxton, you're putting words into my mouth."

Janet pursed her lips. "Suppose we leave it at that, my dear. I didn't believe before in the existence of any such stigma, I now know that most definitely there is such a dreadful thing. It only compounds the entire dreadful experience of dealing with such an illness. For making that clear to me so early on in Kay's illness, then I should, in fact, I do thank you. You may have saved me much heartbreak in the long run. One thing I will say, perhaps to reassure you a little. As far as I know, mental illness, although it can strike anyone, anytime time right out of the blue and often for no apparent reason, is not catching. Now goodbye, and the coffee was on me."

ELEVEN

Taking the Consultant's advice to heart, Janet threw herself into her work, both at school and in spring cleaning her bungalow to within an inch of its life. Day after day, she worked and pushed herself to the point of utter exhaustion in the vain hope that when she got to bed, she would at least get a couple of hours of dreamless sleep.

Forget it, thought Janet. *every sleeping and waking moment is filled to capacity with horrific mental images of my poor daughter being strapped to a cot as she underwent the dreaded ECT. A form of the most hideous torture, for which, God help me, I signed the bloody consent form.*

Even worse was recalling the most recent phone call from her mother up in Scotland who'd said: "Janet, I refuse to hear another minute of this, there's never been any insanity in our family. If as you say, Kay is currently being rather difficult with alarming mood swings, I blame you, you should have been at home to bring up your daughter, rather than going back to teaching and leaving her as a young child to nannies, nurseries and the like especially with her father being at sea for such long absences."

As Janet had tried her best to contest this old-fashioned attitude to a woman's sacred role in life, her Mother equally determined to have the last word said: "You still don't see it, do you? Never wondered why I relocated to Scotland when your father died? No, as a conveniently placed grieving widow, I'd have been in line for the job of bringing up Kay. Well, I reckoned having brought up my own family, cared for your Dad in his last illness, suddenly this was my time to do as I wished for once in my life. The phrase merry widow sprang to mind, so back to Scotland I went to a life that I wished to enjoy. No, Janet, if you want me to spell it out for you then I will, Kay is your daughter. You dragged her up in the way you deemed fitting, so now if she's plaguing you with mood swings and other such nonsense, then no need to put mental illness names on such shenanigans, sheer bad behaviour that's what I'd call it. You may recall the many occasions on which I said: 'Spare the rod and spoil the child', A bit of good old-fashioned discipline, never did you any harm now did it? Any way, you'll have to excuse me but I'm leaving next week for a cruise in the Med and I still have a lot of packing to do."

As the weeks wore on and the news of her daughter's incarceration in a mental hospital became more widely known, Janet was finding in so many insidious ways that more and more people were actively avoiding her. Even worse were those openly apparent times when a so-called friend even one of longstanding, on catching sight of Janet in the near distance would dart into a shop or as had happened on several other occasions, even disappear at high speed up a side street.

So much for friendship, thought Janet. *All right, so where do I go from here? Who can I talk to? Who could possibly help me in this nightmare situation? Suddenly it came to her like a flash Yes, that's it, that's exactly what I'll do. After all, for years now I've been a leading light on the flower rota, and the coffee morning committee. As for helping at jumble sales, at one point I was so involved with them that once I heard someone refer to me as Jumble Janet. Apart from that claim to fame, I am after all a faithful attender at Church every Sunday morning. So, why shouldn't I have a little chat in private with the Vicar?*

Having fully resolved on this course of action, and phoned ahead, when she arrived at the Vicarage that particular Saturday morning, it was to the news that the Vicar was not after all available. Busy writing his sermon for tomorrow, but no real problem as the young Curate would be happy to see her for a coffee in the church hall. Her tale of woe was soon told. In the silence which followed, the fresh-faced young man fiddled with the handle of the coffee cup, but spoke not a word.

Janet had heard that the Curate was a volunteer in the estimable Samaritan organisation to which she had almost had recourse in the dark night of the soul. So if anybody could help her with words of comfort, or help her to understand God's meaning in all of this horrible situation, then surely the Curate could; the right man at the right time.

Feeling her eyes on him, the young man pushed as aside his coffee cup, looked across at Janet and said: "From what you've told me Mrs Caxton, I'd be inclined to say ... that is your cross in life to bear."

Janet could feel her eyes widen in astonishment. "And that, Mr Reid, that is the sum total of your input? This hellish nightmare ... and I use the words advisedly ... this frightful nightmare in which I am currently engulfed ... you, a man of God, all the help you can offer me is to state the obvious that this entire scenario of the damned is my cross in life to bear? Do you think that I am so utterly stupid that I don't already know that? Thanks for nothing and good-day to you."

As she rose to leave the hall, the Curate stretched forth his hand to detain her. "If only you'd let me finish Mrs Caxton."

She shook off his would-be restraining hand. "As far as I'm concerned you have already finished. I'm only glad I didn't waste a phone call to the Samaritans, to you, at three o'clock one morning ... the dark night of the soul, I believe it's called ... three o'clock one morning when I had the bread knife in one hand and a bottle of pills in the other, with my husband somewhere on the high seas. Alone in an empty house with my daughter undergoing the horrors of electro-convulsive therapy. This morning's meeting with you has been a big enough waste of both our times, but I'd have hated more to waste a telephone call to you."

Although he started to speak, Janet would not let him interrupt her flow. "Well, somehow I got through that particular suicidal crisis on my own and I daresay I'll manage again, and totally without any words of so-called comfort from you. Yes, you're so right, my cross in life to bear and believe me, I will bloody well bear it. Goodbye, see you in Church ... or on second thoughts perhaps not."

TWELVE

Her husband was due to arrive home any day now. While she was keenly looking forward to his homecoming, although she had kept him informed of Kay's progress in hospital, as yet, she had not informed him of her own part in signing those accursed consent forms.

I must admit that traumatic as all that was, Kay does now seem to be getting quite a bit better, So far, so good.

I now know how to deal with those noseyparkers. The moment they ask me in tones of doom, "And how is your daughter?" Nowadays I give them absolutely no information, a brisk, "fine thanks" or on occasion vary it to "good days and bad days like all the rest of us." And having said that, leaving them stranded as it were, I immediately bat the question back at them, when being equally solicitous, I ask, "And what about your own family, how are they?"

Janet grinned. Aye, it works every blessed time for let's face it, there isn't a family in the land but what they too have some dirty linen, not suitable for washing in public.

Janet's husband looked across the breakfast table.

"Private joke, is it, or can anyone join in?"

Janet shook her head. "Just a passing thought. Anyway, your first visit yesterday to the hospital went rather well, didn't it?"

He nodded. "Better, much better than I could possibly have imagined. They're doing a grand job there, if in fact Kay really had been as ill latterly as you made out in your letters. What with her manic spending sprees, her navvy's use of obscene language, and of course, escaping from the hospital in her nightie. What with all that, God alone knows what I expected to find."

Janet could feel a tide of anger rising to her cheeks.

"Let us not forget that far from exaggerating her condition in my letters to you, as per usual it was me, alone, that had to bear the brunt of it all at the climax of your beloved daughter's breakdown. Who had the onerous task of leading her into the hospital, like a lamb to the slaughter in the first place so that she could be legally sectioned. Who had to cope when she escaped, then the consent forms for that dreadful treatment?"

He raised his eyes to heaven. "Leave it, Janet, it's over, Kay's on the mend and thank God for it."

She glared at her husband. "Over ? Is it? Is that what you really think? Now that she's been diagnosed, manic-depression, try living with that in the family."

He matched her stare for stare. "At lease it's a degree better than your own amateur diagnosis. As I recall, you had our girl marked down and written off as schizophrenic."

Janet got to her feet. "There is still one other major hurdle, which, as yet, you know nothing about – the attitude of other stupid, scared and ill-informed people. And trust me, that has a very real, very devastating effect. I believe it's known as the on-going stigma of mental illness."

He banged his cup down on the table with such force that it caused the now-empty toast rack to rattle against a plate.

"Stigma? The unwarranted stigma? Oh, come on, that may have been true enough in the bad old days, the days of forbidding Gothic like Victorian Mental Asylums, which also did double duty as Workhouses for the poor, decrepit and decayed homeless. But today, in these enlightened times, with modern hospitals and not a workhouse keeper in sight, surely you must be letting your imagination run away with you, Janet."

She chewed at her lower lip. "Imagination, you say? I'll say no more on the subject, but let's see how you cope when it first happens to you, when a previously trusted friend studiously avoids you, by nipping smartly up a side street rather than greeting you, far less have to talk to you. Let's face it, had Kay been suffering from kidney problems, heart disease, even a broken leg, then it would have been a case of tea and sympathy all round. People can see a broken leg, make a great play of signing the plaster, but a broken shattered mind ... that monstrosity, and everyone in the family in any way connected to it ... to be shunned at all costs, people are then in danger of getting killed in the rush to get away from such a terrible, shamefully embarrassing condition."

He sighed deeply. "Janet, you are certainly overstating the case, reading too much into slights where really no hurt is intended."

She started to gather up the breakfast dishes.

"I'll say no more on the subject. But first time you are at the receiving end of the mental illness stigma, the cold shoulder treatment, believe me, you'll know. See where your high-minded theories get you then."

THIRTEEN

The following Sunday, coming out from the early service Janet and her husband were standing at the top of the stairs chatting to the Vicar, the Curate having bustled past with head bent the very moment he saw Mrs Caxton. Jim spotted someone they both knew approaching the adjoining Church hall.

"Oh, look, Janet, isn't that your teaching protégée, Greta? Do please excuse us, Vicar, but this may be my only chance to meet Greta and her husband before I go back to sea. Old friends, you know, all that sort of thing. Thank you for a lovely service, Vicar."

By the time they had said their goodbyes to other worshippers standing in a row by the doorway and made their way across the car park, Greta and Desmond had disappeared. Intent on his purpose, Jim, not to be outdone, made his way into the Church Hall, assuming that the young couple on coffee-morning rota were setting the scene in readiness for the later service after which many older parishioners usually welcomed a cuppa and a bit of a natter with people they would not again meet until the following week. Once inside the hall, Janet and her husband stopped short at the scene which met their eyes. Long trestle tables had been joined together, draped in fancy lace cloths, in front of each chair and place setting could be seen an elegantly wrought place card and centre stage was a beautifully decorated christening cake. They were still gazing at this party-setting when Greta, Desmond and another couple of Janet's erstwhile friends and school colleagues came chattering and laughing from the kitchen area beyond the partition. As if a tap had been turned off, the carefree laughter didn't even die away gradually, instead it stopped dead when the four young people came face-to-face with Janet and her husband. The first to recover his equilibrium was Captain Jim, who in his usual astute manner had summed up the embarrassing situation in one single, mental leap. Given that in his line of work, he was always the one in charge and never one to mince his words, he at once assumed full command. Having wordlessly but pointedly looked all around the hall, then looked the work party up and down, as if on Captain's inspection, he finally spoke directly to Greta and her husband.

"So, It's your son's christening today, a happy family occasion. You may recall, Greta, that in the absence of your own father – who in order to go off with another woman, had abandoned you and your mother – in his absence, it was I who, dressed overall, as you requested in my best Naval uniform, did the honours in walking you down the aisle. That too was a very happy family event. But then nothing stays the same for ever, families, people, events move on, nothing is set in concrete."

Janet, close to tears and fearful of what else her husband would say, laid a restraining hand on his arm. He turned his head at the slight movement, gently took hold of her hand and tucking it into his arm, he gave a sad little smile to the assembled group.

"Seems my dear wife is reminding me ... we too have a family appointment this afternoon, the visiting hour at the Nerve Hospital. As yet, you may not have heard on the local grapevine, but our darling daughter, Kay, has a mental illness for which she is currently being treated. And that's where our priorities now lie, so even had we received an invitation to the christening party ... doubtless lost in the post ... I'd imagine, we would have had to decline."

As Janet and her husband, their heads held high, their body language shrieking defiance, made their way out of the hall, somehow the former air of festivity and good cheer had evaporated. Holding tight to Jim's arm, Janet whispered: "Well done. You've lost your vocation as a ship's Captain, you'd make a great Shakespearian actor."

A Daughter is for Life

Her husband laughed out loud. "And if it's tragedy on the grand scale you want, that too can be arranged, just one word from you on the subject of mental illness stigma, unwarranted or otherwise, then murder will be done."

In the wake of the non-invitation to the christening party, and although with the hurt going too deep, neither Janet nor Jim ever referred to it again, nevertheless it had left an indelible mark on their minds and on their lives.

"Well, dear, what do you think? Should I give up seafaring? You could leave your school and those colleagues that you thought were firm friends. We could sell up here and once Kay is out of hospital after her quota of trial weekends at home, we could relocate, perhaps to Scotland, live nearby your mother, that would be a help, and you'd like that wouldn't you, dear?"

Janet gazed in wonder. "Relocate to Scotland, be nearer to my mother? Why on earth should I want that? Honestly do you even read the letters I send you, or perhaps some of them have not turned up. Thing is, these days, my mother is scarcely speaking to me, yes, another outcome of Kay's illness, my mother blames me for the nightmare illness."

She stopped to draw breath. "All right, I could teach as well there as here in England. But what about you, how do you propose to earn an honest crust? Somehow, I just do not see you as an impoverished feather-duster wielding househusband."

He gave a tut of annoyance. "No, no, my dear, nor do I. Rather I was thinking along the lines of using our savings and the money from the sale of the house to buy a little sub-post office, perhaps one with a house or cottage attached, maybe even an outhouse we could convert into a tearoom."

Not wishing to dampen his enthusiasm, but still fully alert to the stark reality of their family situation, Janet said: "I don't know that my baking skills are up to that and what you know about being a postmaster could be written on a postage stamp. Perhaps best to wait and see what Kay's psychiatrist makes of it all."

Having made a splendid recovery and with her mood swings now moderated and reasonably controlled by the precise amount of correct medication, Kay set about trying to rebuild any sort of meaningful life for herself. Before she was finally released from hospital, there were several family consultations with the team of excellent psychiatrists whose expertise had brought her to such near-miraculous recovery.

Janet and Jim were told: "From here on Kay must be allowed to make her own way in life, make her own decisions, live independently and free of the family home. And remembering that each and every one of you have been traumatised by the events, the same freedom of action must also be given to you, as the parents."

Captain Jim glanced across at his wife, knowing full well that such a plan was in direct opposition to what they themselves had previously been discussing in private.

Catching this look between husband and wife, Mr Swanwick said: "Yes, I do know it is your natural instinct is to want to protect your daughter, to wrap her in cotton wool, more or less for the rest of her life. But trust me and I do speak from many years experience of treating this type of illness, the mother hen approach would not work. Rather it would become a tightly-knotted life-sentence for all three of you. Over time it would strangle all initiative, all creative thought, all freedom, and eventually suck every iota of the life force from each one of you."

A stunned silence greeted this until it was further pointed out to them: "As of now, Kay must have the freedom to make her own decisions and learn to take whatever consequences, be they good, bad or downright horrendous that come in their wake. She must make a fresh start in life, but definitely outwith the family home. And of course, you two, as a married couple, you must get your own life back on track. Remember although you are parents, you are also two individuals with lives to lead and to enjoy."

As they made their way home with Kay for yet another trial weekend, they knew there was much to discuss before they each faced the next stage of their onward journey. As they again entered the family bungalow, Janet laughed.

"As my dear old Scottish Granny used to say, 'What's for ye, will no go by ye', whatever that means, but at least it sounds positive , so do we positively return to Scotland or equally positively stay down here in England, but doing what?"

FOURTEEN

The last of the trial weekends had come, amazingly with a certain measure of success. With Kay now due to be out of hospital within a matter of days, more and more urgent was the cry: "Where to go from here?"

A great theory, keep her away from the family home, but how to achieve this miracle?

Janet had the glimmer of an idea. "That other woman I met one day in the hospital canteen Wendy's mother. Like Kay, Wendy's now much better and will also be out soon. So Mrs Turner is in the same dilemma as us."

Jim nodded. "So why not give her a call?"

On the Wednesday evening Val Turner and her husband duly arrived at the Caxton's bungalow. Over coffee, the two couples were soon deeply into what was uppermost in all their minds. Strangely enough the Turners had been thinking along the same lines as had Janet and Jim.

"It's going to be one hell of an upheaval, selling up, moving to another district or another country, changing our lives around. But like you, we want the best for our daughter and one thing on which we're adamant ..."

Jim leant forward. "Let me guess ... no way are you allowing your daughter to relocate into some sort of half-way community hostel with a load of former patients, right?"

Val nodded. "I think we're all agreed on that one. But like you, as responsible and caring parents, we are determined to make whatever sacrifice is necessary, if it helps our daughter's complete recovery."

There were nods of agreement all round, then Janet spoke up, "You know, there's a couple of things occur to me ... perhaps you'd all bear with me while I try to explain my rather jumbled thoughts in some semblance of clarity ..."

Forefinger to her cheek and a look of intense concentration on her face, Janet said: "Let's see now, when I was a girl growing up in Glasgow in the years of the great Depression, often I would see adults holding whispered conversations behind cupped hands. Some terrible scandal you might think? News of a vicious stabbing or gang fights in the neighbourhood? Nothing so dramatic. They were discussing that which must at all costs be told only in secret ... an illness. So shameful was it that nobody ever said the actual word, but whispered only the letters TB. Yes, although nobody ever said the dreaded word tuberculosis, the fact was that the illness was then prevalent throughout the City of Glasgow. The whispered TB was to inform neighbours of which poor soul had become its latest victim. Talk about secrecy, shame, scandal ... and above all stigma. Do you see what I'm driving at?"

Bill Turner nodded. "Nowadays people talk openly about tuberculosis but not about mental illness."

"That's right," said Janet. "So why should we all have to endure the unwarranted stigma of mental illness? And if we all run away, we're helping to keep the stigma alive and well. Why not stay, fight our corner, look the world in the face, talk about the unmentionable illness. Talk about the devastating effect it has, not just on the patient, but on his or her family. At least if we have the courage of our convictions we all keep our own self-respect. Perhaps even more important, this way, we'd know who our real friends are."

"All very well in theory, I daresay, but one thing you're forgetting, Janet. That still leaves us with a rather difficult daughter in the family home. Exactly what the psychiatrists have advised us not to do. And, I suppose, like me, you also, Janet, have found that when the behaviour is at its worst, when times are really bloody, downright horrendous, it's then that their nearest and dearest are left to take the flak."

Janet gave a bitter laugh. "Amen to that and that was the other point I wanted to address with you. For it is a definite facet of mental illness that the people they love the most, those are the very people they turn against. And, of course, in our case, with daughters, it's poor old Mum who gets the worst of it, isn't that so, Val?

Jim leant forward. "In that case why don't we work out a swap or some sort of exchange rota, and help each other in this way?"

Val smiled. "You know, I do believe that would work, the girls have already made friends with each other, being in the same ward."

Bill pursed his lips. "So far so good, but what about jobs, any bright ideas there?"

Another silence, then Val said, "I have a cousin, who once had a nervous breakdown. She holds to the view it can happen to anybody. She now owns a little teashop in Harborne village, she's been very supportive to us. I daresay, she could always use another couple of waitresses or dishwashers. What do you all think?"

Jim got to his feet. "I think we've had enough coffee for one night, something stronger now called for and perhaps a toast, 'The stigma, who the hell cares and anyway who needs it?'."

Bill Turner laughed. "Sounds good, Jim, but if you'd let me propose a wonderful toast I've just been learning in my night school Spanish class, Val thought it would take my mind off our worries if I learnt another language, so might as well put it to good use, don't you think?"

As they raised well-filled wine glasses, Bill Turner stood up.

"Salud, amor y pesetas y tiempo para gustar."

Val laughed. "Sure sounds very impressive, but for lesser mortals, do please translate."

Jim went and stood beside Bill; together with deep conviction in their voices they said: "Here's to health, love and money and time to enjoy them."

With tears in their eyes, Val and Janet looked across at each other and Janet said: "We may have a long and still bumpy road ahead of us, but with our heads held high and good friends, real friends by our side, who could ask for anything more than, 'Health, Love and Money and Time to enjoy them'."

Who could ask for anything more?

THE END

Jenny Telfer Chaplin